NOISES IN THE NIGHT

by
Kenneth Ireland

℞
RAVETTE PUBLISHING

First published by Ravette Publishing 2001

_____

Printed and bound in Great Britain
for Ravette Publishing Limited,
Unit 3, Tristar Centre,
Star Road, Partridge Green,
West Sussex RH13 8RA
by Cox & Wyman Ltd, Reading, Berkshire

ISBN: 1 84161 031 3

CONTENTS

NOISES
IN THE NIGHT

Jessica didn't sleep very well. She said so at breakfast, when they asked.

"I suppose it was the birds that woke you," said her mother.

"You must expect to hear birds first thing in the morning when you're staying in a village," her father grunted.

"It wasn't the birds," retorted Jessica. "It was somebody walking about most of the night, making groaning noises."

Mrs Hedges, the landlady, came in with a big pot of coffee.

"Jessica's just been telling us she kept hearing noises last night," said her mother.

"It was just somebody walking about upstairs," said Jessica, trying to make it sound less like a complaint.

Mrs Hedges looked at her curiously.

"There wasn't anybody about that I know of," she said, "not after the bar closed, anyway."

"I think it was somebody in the room just above mine," said Jessica.

"There isn't a room above yours," Mrs Hedges said. "There's only the roof. Perhaps it was a squirrel. They can sometimes find their way into the lofts around here."

She put the coffee pot down.

"After you've had your breakfast, I'll get Mr Hedges to come up and have a little listen with you to see what he makes of it," she told her. "There are still a few things we haven't sorted out yet. We've only been here a month. In fact, you're our first guests since we moved in."

She smiled round at them.

"So apart from the noise, is everything else all right?"

Everything else was fine. It was a pretty little village. Even from Jessica's quite small bedroom, there was a view over the entire countryside with lots of fields and woods, and plenty of other interesting villages around to visit during the day.

They had arrived there almost by accident. Jessica's parents had decided that this year they would simply load the car, drive south until they found somewhere they liked, then wherever it was, stay for just a few days before moving on again.

They had all liked the look of the quaint old country pub and, when they saw the large card in the window offering bed and breakfast, had gone in to enquire about accommodation. There were only two guest bedrooms, so her parents had taken one, and Jessica had been put in the other.

As promised, after breakfast, Mr Hedges went upstairs with her and they stood together in her room listening intently. Neither of them could hear anything now. Jessica mentioned the squirrels.

"Too high off the ground for them, I would have thought," Mr Hedges said thoughtfully.

Jessica glanced up at the ceiling. Just behind the door was a small trapdoor, freshly painted like the rest of the room. A squirrel couldn't have got up through there, though. They both listened carefully again.

"Well, there doesn't seem to be anything up there now," said Mr Hedges. "But if you do hear it again, let me know and I'll go up with a torch and take a good look round. I've been too busy redecorating and putting new furniture in to climb up there yet. This room hadn't been used for years before we came, not since Mrs Hedge's grandfather slept in it."

"Her grandfather? Is this where he died?" she asked anxiously, immediately thinking of ghosts.

"No. He just disappeared," said Mr Hedges.

She looked at him in disbelief.

"Really disappeared?" she asked.

Mr Hedges shrugged.

"Seems so. At any rate, nobody's seen him since. Of course that was a good few years ago. Then some sort of cousin took the pub over, and now it's passed down to us. Lucky it did, in a way. I'd just been made redundant from work when it happened."

"When what happened?" asked Jessica. She had an awful thought now that perhaps it had been the cousin's ghost she had heard instead.

"He disappeared as well," said Mr Hedges, casually. "You'd hardly credit it, would you – two in one family, so to speak? It was quite a shock when we heard, especially since my wife had kept in touch, being the nearest relative. In fact she'd visited him here only a few days before. Still, that's nothing for you to worry about."

This was fascinating, Jessica decided, as they went back down the stairs. Nobody had ever told her interesting things like this whenever they had stayed in a hotel.

"You shouldn't listen to gossip," her mother said when she gave them the news.

"I didn't ask him about it," she protested. "He just told me."

Before she went to bed that night, she

looked round the room carefully. She supposed there had always been a bed in the room where hers was now. It was about the only place one would fit. She supposed the old man had slept just where she did.

Or would the landlady's grandfather really have been an old man when he disappeared? Perhaps he wasn't, not at the time. Perhaps he'd only be an old man now – if he was still alive, of course, and that was unlikely after all these years.

No grandfather's ghost, then, that was for certain: He hadn't died here, he'd just vanished, like that cousin, and that was quite a different matter. Funny two people should just disappear like that, though. She wondered what the police had made of it.

She went to bed.

The noises started again not long afterwards. She listened carefully. It didn't sound like squirrels to her at all. The sounds were too heavy, for one thing, and definitely like footsteps – dragging ones, she decided after a few more minutes.

Then the scratching began and Jessica was fairly sure she could hear that groaning again, but only every now and then. It might just have been the wind, she thought, blowing round the old chimney stacks.

The groaning stopped. Then the scratching. Now she could only hear the strange footstep-like sounds, moving slowly up and down over her head. It was very annoying. If she could get closer to the ceiling she might have a better idea of what was causing it.

Jessica switched on her bedside light and looked at the trapdoor in the ceiling. That would be the best place to listen, if only she could get up to it. She got out of bed, moved one of the two wooden chairs in her room directly beneath the trapdoor and stood on it.

It was not really high enough. She got down, moved the chair aside and carefully dragged the little dressing-table from against the wall and stood on that instead. This was better! Now she could touch the trapdoor with both hands, and could hear the noises a little more clearly – but still not sufficiently well to make them out properly.

Perhaps if she pushed the trapdoor up, just a little bit, and then listened ... After all, there couldn't be anything big and dangerous up there or it couldn't have got into the roof space in the first place.

The trapdoor was stuck because of the new paint Mr Hedges had put on it when he redecorated the room. She thumped at it a little trying to make it open, hoping not to make too much noise. Oddly, the noises in the loft stopped immediately.

She kept still for a moment, listening. Whatever was up there seemed to have gone.

Unless there had been nothing there in the first place, and she'd only been hearing gurgling from the old water pipes, or something like that.

Unless it really was a squirrel, or even a whole family of them which Mr Hedges hadn't discovered yet. She didn't think it could be bats. Bats didn't walk about.

Now the noises had stopped again, she got down and put everything back where it belonged. Then she climbed back into bed and went to sleep.

The noises woke her again not long afterwards. They sounded louder this time, exactly like someone pacing about on bare boards just above her head.

She sat up. This was really annoying now. If she was going to get any sleep at all, something would have to be done about this. She put the light back on, opened the door and stepped out into the corridor.

There she hesitated while she thought about the best thing to do. Telling her parents was likely to be a waste of time. After all, she couldn't move in with them for the rest of the night because she knew there wasn't a spare bed in their room. She didn't fancy sleeping on the floor. Neither did she fancy wandering round the empty pub in her nightie trying to find Mr and Mrs Hedges.

She went back inside her room and closed the door. She'd just have to see if she could sort this out for herself. She dragged the dressing-table under the trapdoor again, climbed up and slapped at it angrily with both hands.

The noises stopped again straight away. Good! That seemed to have scared whatever was up there. It certainly couldn't have been anything to do with gurgling water pipes. She was fairly certain now it had to be a squirrel – or rats, though she hoped not.

She could imagine a rat hiding at the far end of the loft, ready to scamper further away if she hit the trapdoor again. After all, there must be a hole somewhere for it to make its escape.

She slapped both hands against the flap a few more times, rather harder this time, to encourage it to leave. That was when the trapdoor suddenly tilted sideways and stuck, half-open and half-closed.

She looked at it cautiously. She thought she'd better not leave it like that, or they'd certainly know she'd been climbing on the furniture. It couldn't have got like that by itself.

She listened again, first to make quite sure the creature that had been up there had really gone. Then she carefully pushed the trapdoor all the way up with both hands, fingers spread to keep it level while she lowered it properly back into place.

There was a thump followed by a slithering noise just above her head. Suddenly the trapdoor rose from her hands and with a loud clatter fell to one side.

To her horror, she found an old wrinkled face with blackened teeth and curling wet lips scowling down at her from the blackness of the loft and she could smell foul breath.

Before she could cry out, dark hands were reaching down towards her, clamping themselves round her head and dragging her upwards.

The bedroom door burst open. To her relief she saw Mrs Hedges, in her nightie and dressing gown, standing there.

"Help me!" gasped Jessica, feebly.

Mrs Hedges hurried towards her at once. Jessica felt her hands gripping her. But instead of pulling her free, they were underneath her, pushing her fiercely upwards.

Soon the only sounds to be heard in the room were footsteps dragging across the ceiling, a scratching sound, then what might have been groans.

Then silence.

"Goodnight, grandfather," said Mrs Hedges softly, as the flap dropped quietly back into place. "That should keep you going for a while."

Then she closed the door quietly

behind her and went back along the corridor.
Now Jessica had disappeared as well.

THE MONSTER UNDER THE BED

Megan was peering cautiously into her wardrobe when her mother suddenly came into her room.

"Why aren't you in bed?" said her mother. "What are you doing?"

"Nothing. Just looking in my wardrobe," mumbled Megan.

"Well, whatever it is you're looking for, you can find it in the morning," said her mother firmly. "It's late. Get to bed."

Megan closed the wardrobe door and turned the key before obediently scurrying to her bed and tucking herself in.

"Now go to sleep," said her mother, turning out the light and shutting the door behind her.

Megan's mother had interrupted a necessary routine which she performed every night.

The first essential was to make sure that there was nothing but clothes inside her wardrobe, and to be ready to lock it at once if she found anything else. (And then lock it anyway!)

Tonight that was as far as she had got before her mother had come in so unexpectedly. So she quietly got out of bed and switched the light back on again.

Now she had to make sure that her curtains were tightly drawn so that if the monster did happen to be lurking outside, it wouldn't be able to see where she slept.

Next she had to look under her bed. Almost all the available space was already taken up with boxes full of her old books and toys, but she still had to be quite sure.

After that, the routine demanded that she went over to the door, paused for a final careful check round the room before turning off the light, running quickly to her bed, leaping into it and tucking the bedclothes in all round as fast as she could.

Now she must lie perfectly still because at this point she had to hold her breath for as long as possible. That was because the monster could detect the movement of her chest while she was breathing and so might still find her.

She knew that eventually it would either give up or go away, and only then would it be quite safe to go to sleep.

It was the same every night. It was worrying, knowing there was a monster about and that there wasn't very much she could do about it, apart from take these precautions.

Her brother Edward had told her she was being stupid. That was the night he had just been going to bed himself, had heard her rushing about in her room and had gone in to find out what she was up to.

"There couldn't be a monster under your bed," he had said, scornfully. "Go on, take a good look and see for yourself."

"I just have," she told him. That was what she had been doing as he came in.

"Then look again. Go on."

"Keep your voice down, or it'll hear us," Megan had said anxiously.

Actually, she was more cross that her brother had discovered her secret nightly routine.

"All right," he whispered, "I will, but just think for once. How could a monster get under your bed with all that rubbish under it already? There isn't room for anything else."

"It isn't rubbish," Megan had defended. "It's all sorts of things I've had for a long time and want to keep."

"Whatever," retorted Edward. "Anyway, you can see now that nothing else could be under there as well, can't you?"

Rather reluctantly, Megan had to agree. Expecting to find a monster under her bed really didn't make much sense, at all.

"See?" said Edward. "And why would a monster be hiding in your wardrobe? In fact how does it get into the house in the first place?"

"It comes up through the little gaps between the floorboards," she decided.

"How could it?" Edward demanded.

"It just does."

"Then it must be a very tiny monster if it can do that," said Edward scornfully. "So tiny, in fact, you'd be able to beat the daylights out of it as soon as you saw it, wouldn't you?" he added.

Then he went all round the room pointing out there was nowhere else a monster could hide, trying to convince her there was nothing to worry about, especially as, she'd never actually *seen* a monster in her room.

"I wouldn't be able to in the dark," objected Megan.

"You wouldn't be able to see one in broad daylight either," said Edward. "Because there are no such things as monsters, so you might as well forget it. You're just being silly."

Megan didn't think he'd told their parents her secret. They never said anything, anyway. And Edward had never mentioned it again either.

But Edward was wrong. There was a monster! She didn't know how, but she knew there was one and the only thing she could do about it was carry on taking her usual precautions and hope for the best, no matter what Edward said.

At least doing that kept it away, or out of sight, which was almost as good.

In fact, everything would have been all right if a few nights later, Edward hadn't given her a fright by suddenly bursting into her room. She was almost asleep at the time.

When he switched on her light she could see he was white-faced and trembling and leaning against the door to make sure it stayed shut.

"What's the matter? Is the house on fire?" she asked sleepily.

"No. There really is a monster, just like you said. It nearly got me!" he said breathlessly.

"It can't have," she said, sitting up.

"It did! I'd just gone to sleep when something grabbed hold of me and started pulling me out of bed. I had to struggle really hard before I got away. I couldn't see what it looked like in the dark, but it wasn't tiny at all. It was enormous!"

That was a surprise. Edward being so scared, but almost satisfying in a way. Usually he was always so calm about everything. She considered carefully for a moment.

"Then it couldn't have come up through your floorboards, because you've got a fitted carpet, and I haven't. I expect it was hiding in your wardrobe all the time, waiting for you to go to sleep. Then as soon as it knew you were, it crept out, then ..."

"It couldn't have been in my wardrobe. I checked that before I got into bed."

That was a surprise as well.

"So it must have come up through the floorboards in my room, then when it couldn't find me in the dark, slid through the crack under the door and went into your room instead," she said, very matter-of-fact. "Why didn't you shout for Mum and Dad?"

"I was too scared to shout. Besides, they wouldn't have believed me."

No, they wouldn't, thought Megan. She didn't suppose their parents would have understood at all.

"Was it a really cold hand that grabbed you?" she asked thoughtfully.

"No. Not really. I'm not even sure it was a hand. It felt scaly."

"So now you know," said Megan, nodding. Just what she'd always suspected. "Then what?"

"It dragged me across the carpet and as far as the wall before I managed to escape." Edward was still gasping in panic.

"It was probably going to pull you all the way through the wall and right outside the house, then," said Megan. "Then eat you in the garden, I expect. You were lucky to get away." She thought again for a moment. "So where is it now?"

Edward stared at her.

"It must still be in my room!"

Megan shook her head.

"I don't think so. I think it's only here in the dark, otherwise we'd be able to see it all the time. If you managed to switch your light on, I expect it would just disappear."

Edward had calmed down a bit by now.

"How do you know?" he asked.

Megan considered. She just knew. That was what monsters did. They were never there when the light was on, or in daylight. They were only dangerous when you were in bed, or if you didn't switch the light on while you went upstairs.

"It'll be all right now," she said confidently. "It'll have gone by now."

Edward opened her door and looked out cautiously. She heard him a few seconds later noisily switching on the light in his room. Then there was the unmistakable creak of his wardrobe door as he opened it, then another creak as he shut it again, then a few thumps as he shot rapidly back into bed.

She lay awake for a while, staring into the darkness. She had never found a monster hiding in her wardrobe, even though she searched every night.

Not that she really knew what a monster would look like. Something big, she expected, a bit like a gorilla but more like a reptile, with three enormous claws on each hand. Edward had said it felt scaly. That fitted.

She had never actually noticed one lurking outside her window when it was dark, before pulling her curtains tight so it couldn't see in. So, even if it did wait outside until then, it wouldn't come in and hide in her wardrobe. At least, she didn't think so, but she'd still carry on looking every night, just in case!

It had to have found some secret way of getting into the house every night, then waiting under the floorboards until it was dark in her room. It was obvious now. That was why she had never found it under her bed. She should have realised sooner.

The only problem with that was, if it was as big as Edward said, how did it manage to squeeze its way past the floorboards? There was total silence in the house now. Edward must have gone to sleep again, she decided. She was almost asleep herself. Then she was.

She woke later in the night. It was

dark. She was sure she could hear a movement somewhere in her room, something sidling towards her bed!

She lay perfectly still, listening intently. Then something brushed past her bedclothes. Then slithered near her wardrobe. Then the sound stopped. It had gone.

She waited a few seconds to make quite certain about that before sitting up, then after a few more seconds dashed over to the light switch. She'd be safe with the light on. She knew that, just as very young children know when their parents leave a little light on, it's safe to go to sleep.

But this was totally unexpected, all of it. She hadn't expected Edward to start looking for monsters as well, still less to be dragged out of bed by one.

Perhaps he hadn't, of course. Most likely he'd been dreaming at the time and just thought he had. After all, while a monster might seem real enough while she was making sure there wasn't one in her room, common sense told her there wasn't a monster there at all.

Not that she was going to tell anyone else that. She just made quite sure each night, that was all. So it was a great surprise and, rather alarming, to have heard what must have been a monster in her room just now, even if it was no longer there.

She looked down at the floor. There was a tiny gap under her door. So could it really ... ? And, if so, as Edward had pointed out about the floorboards, how ... ?

She opened her door and looked out. Edward's door was just slightly open. Strange. He usually kept it shut. Perhaps he'd started leaving it like that recently so people could hear him shout if he had to.

Well, she might as well satisfy her curiosity. Boldly she turned off her light, went to his door, pushed it wide open, and went into his room.

The monster had come back! Megan could just make out Edward struggling on the floor with it standing over him. He wasn't able to shout out because one of the monster's scaly hands was clamped firmly over his mouth.

Megan dashed forward bravely.

"Get off him!" she said angrily. "Leave him alone!"

The monster, nearly as high as the ceiling, brushed her aside and began to drag her brother towards the door. Then it went through it – and into her room!

Megan chased after them both, anxiously trying to pull her brother from the monster's grip. At last she tried to shout for help, but now found she was unable to make a sound.

The only thing she could do now was

carry on struggling with it. She supposed this was how a monster always captured its victim, by somehow making it impossible to call for help.

Now Edward had been pulled to the side of her bed and, still struggling, he disappeared under it.

That was when, even in the dark, Megan suddenly realised just how the monster was able to come up between the gaps in the floorboards and, how it could now go back down again, taking Edward with it ...

She watched in horror as they both disappeared. Then, finally she switched the light back on. The room was empty. There was nothing she could do now. She switched the light off again, and scrambled into bed.

Well, there would certainly be a lot of questions in the morning if Edward was still missing. She would be asked if she knew what had happened to him. She decided she wouldn't say anything. After all, as they had both agreed, parents never understood this sort of thing at all.

Besides, it was likely he would be back again by the morning, remembering nothing about it. She wouldn't be entirely surprised. She might even have found she'd dreamt the whole thing. But if not, when morning came she'd soon find out.

Either way, she would continue to

carry on taking her nightly precautions, particularly now she knew what could happen if she didn't.

After all, she had never really believed that a monster would come into her room in the first place, but then, neither had Edward, until she had explained it to him.

FAIRIES AT THE BOTTOM OF THE GARDEN

"We've got fairies," announced Becky proudly.

"That's nice, dear," said Mrs Herbert, carrying on with her knitting as she sat in the big arm chair. Mrs Herbert was Becky's grandmother, who was visiting.

"I've just been to see them," persisted Becky. "They're still there," she added.

"And what do they look like?" asked her grandmother. "Are they pretty, with gossamer wings?"

Becky was scornful.

"Some of them might be pretty, I suppose, but of course they haven't got wings."

"I thought all fairies had wings," was Mrs Herbert's comment.

"Ours don't."

Becky's mother came in.

"Stop pestering your poor grand-mother," she said.

"She's no trouble," said Grandma Herbert. "She was just telling me about the fairies. It's nice to see a child of her age with such a lively imagination. Where did you see them, then?" she asked Becky, turning her head towards the little girl and smiling encouragingly.

"At the bottom of the garden," replied Becky, "just the other side of the cold frame. They live in some of the plant pots."

Her grandmother nodded.

"Exactly where anyone might expect to find them," she said, almost as if she thought if perfectly natural to find fairies at the bottom of the garden.

"She's been on about them for weeks now. Don't encourage her," warned Becky's mother, "or she'll start to believe they're really there."

"They *are* really there," protested Becky. "I go and see them every day, except when it's raining."

Becky's mother raised her eyes to heaven as she looked at Mrs Herbert, who caught the glance and nodded with a slight smile on her face.

"Well, it's not raining now, so do you think I might be able to see them?" asked Becky's grandmother, slyly.

"Oh no. They won't come out for you."

"Don't be rude, Becky," said her mother, putting Mrs Herbert's cup of coffee on the table at the side of her.

"I'm not being rude. They won't. It's because they don't know you, you see." Grandma Herbert didn't visit them very often.

"Then while my coffee cools, let's go outside and then you can show me where you see them," said Mrs Herbert, putting down her knitting and getting to her feet.

Becky scampered out through the kitchen door and along the path which ran alongside the garden to the rockery at the far end. Then she disappeared behind the rockery.

Mrs Herbert who had followed much more slowly, found her granddaughter pointing excitedly at a spot near the fence, just beyond the cold frame.

"They're in there," she said.

Her grandmother peered at the overgrown jumble of old plant pots, bits of wood and chunks of spare rock left over from when the rockery had been built.

"I can't see them," she said, bending down.

"You mustn't poke," instructed Becky. "You'll upset them. How would you like it if someone poked at your home?"

"I don't think they can be very

comfortable in there," remarked her grandmother. "In fact, I think you might be telling fibs," she added, straightening up again.

"I'm not. And they're perfectly comfortable."

"How do you know?" asked her grandmother.

"They told me."

"I've never heard of fairies who talked to humans before," Mrs Herbert commented sharply.

"Mine do. Of course they sound a bit squeaky, but that's because they're so small."

"You're making it all up," decided Mrs Herbert. "You want to be careful, as your mother said, or before you know it, you'll really start to think that what you're pretending is real."

"They are real!" shouted Becky crossly.

Mrs Herbert regarded her coolly.

"I won't believe that until I see them myself," she said. "Fairies are – an invention, that's all. Like in fairy stories. They aren't real, Becky, so it's no use pretending they are. You'll have to learn to grow out of this nonsense."

"It's not nonsense! They are real! They've even asked if I'd like to join them," said Becky doggedly. "I'm thinking about it," she added.

"Very well, Becky," said Grandma Herbert, kindly. "How big are these fairies, since you're so certain about them?"

"About this big," said Becky, extending the finger and thumb of her right hand and showing her.

Mrs Herbert looked at the plant pots. Becky had really got this worked out, she had to admit. The size she was demonstrating meant that her imaginary little creatures would easily fit into the larger plant pots.

"But how could you join them?" persisted her grandmother. "You couldn't possibly fit inside one of those pots, could you? I mean, just look how big you are, then at the size you've just shown me. In any case," she added, "living in there would be all very well, but what would you eat?"

"The same as they do of course."

"And what's that?"

"I don't know. They haven't told me yet. I'll have to ask them. But I'd fit in there with them, because they've already said they know how to make me smaller."

Mrs Herbert sighed. It was no use arguing with her. Becky obviously had everything worked out – quite clever of her, really, at her age – so it was clear everyone would have to wait until she had grown out of this phase.

"Well, when they move on," commented Mrs Herbert, "and go and live in somebody else's garden, don't be disappointed when they vanish." She decided that was the best approach. No point in being too harsh with the child. "Now come and show me the rest of the garden," she added encouragingly.

Becky obediently led the way back to the lawn and the flower beds.

"And that's a fairy ring," she announced pointing to where the grass had formed a circle on the lawn.

Her grandmother bent down to examine it.

"I'd say that's caused by a fungus in the grass," she said. "That's the usual reason for them, anyway."

"Oh no, the grass is flattened in the middle because that's where they come out and dance. They only do it when there's no moon, though, because then they know people won't be able to see them."

Yes. She'd worked out every detail of her fantasy, thought Mrs Herbert to herself. Best not to mention fairies again, if possible. Then she'd soon forget all about them. She'd have a quiet word with Becky's mother about that as soon as the chance presented itself.

The reason Mrs Herbert was there at all was because of the party. She had arrived a day early and stayed overnight because of the distance she had to travel. It was Becky's father's thirty-fifth birthday, and all his friends and relations had been invited.

Later that afternoon they started to arrive. Cars drew up in the drive and the overflow parked on the road outside and the guests climbed out smiling.

Becky was now in her best party frock, standing outside the front door so they would all be sure to notice her.

"Hello, Becky," called Uncle Mike. "How are your fairies?"

"Very well, thank you," said Becky politely.

Uncle Mike and Aunty Irene both gave her a kiss before going inside. He was carrying a small box, wrapped in paper and tied with coloured ribbon. Becky was curious to know what it could be. It was bound to be something expensive. Uncle Mike and Aunty Irene always gave expensive presents.

Then some of her father's business friends and their wives turned up carrying their gifts. They didn't know her very well, so she didn't get a kiss from any of them. Not that she wanted one, anyway.

Then grumpy Grandma and Grandad Jones arrived. Grandma Jones asked if she was behaving herself as she leaned forward for Becky to kiss her, just a peck on the cheek. Grandad Jones just nodded and grunted.

Far too much kissing anyway, decided Becky. She went back into the house before anyone else came. She wanted to see what was in that box. That would be much more interesting than just standing there showing off her party dress. She hoped her father would already have unwrapped it.

She was in luck. Her father had not only unwrapped it, but was examining it in delight. It was a camcorder, the very latest model. She'd seen them in shop windows, and knew her father had wanted one for a long time.

"After you've taken a film you can view it straight away without even attaching it to a television, if you want to check what you've got," Uncle Mike was saying proudly. "Go on, Harry, film something. It focusses automatically, so you don't need to fiddle with anything. Then press that button there, then that one, and look into the viewfinder."

Her father put his eye to the viewfinder, switched on, and moved it slowly round the room. Then he stopped it, wound the film back, and did as his brother-in-law had told him. Becky watched very carefully. The camcorder was so dainty, it could be held in just one hand.

"Very clever," announced Becky's father. "Just the sort of thing I've always wanted. Thanks a lot, Mike. And you, of course, Irene."

"We thought you'd like it," said Aunty Irene happily.

"Let me see!" said Becky eagerly.

Her father held the camcorder to her eye and showed her.

"That's clever!" Becky declared. "Can I have a go?"

Her father looked very doubtful, but Uncle Mike was encouraging.

"Why not?" he said. "She can't break it unless she drops it."

"All right," said her father rather reluctantly. "But not for long. I want to film the party once everyone's arrived." He looked around. "Come with me into the garden and you can use it there, but just for a minute, mind."

Once they were standing on the lawn, her father handed it to her.

"Now to start filming, you press that button there. Then when you've finished – "

"I know," Becky interrupted excitedly. "I was watching when Uncle Mike showed you."

She put the eyepiece to her eye.

"Stand there," she said, "and I'll film you. Move about a bit, though, or it'll be just like taking an ordinary photograph, won't it?"

She pointed the camcorder towards him, while he walked rather self-consciously backwards and forwards.

Then her mother was at the kitchen door.

"Harry," she called – "telephone! It's

Edwin."

"You bring it back inside for me," he told Becky, hurrying towards the house.

Becky kept filming him as he hurried away. Then she stopped the film and looked around for something else which might be interesting. Suddenly she had an idea ...

Later, Grandma Herbert felt a hand tugging at her skirt, as she was talking to one of her son-in-law's business friends. When she looked down in some irritation, she found it was Becky trying to attract her attention.

"I've photographed them," said Becky proudly.

"Photographed what, dear?"

"The fairies, of course. You can see them now if you like." She held up the camcorder for inspection.

"Not just now, dear, I'm talking. Run along."

"Fairies?" said the man, laughing loudly. "What nonsense!"

"Just a ridiculous phase she's going through," Becky heard her grandmother say. "Now you were saying – ?"

Rather crestfallen, Becky hung around for a few moments, but obviously they weren't going to pay any more attention to her. Even Uncle Mike, when she held the camcorder up to him, glanced at it briefly then said:

"Oh, just put it over there 'til your father's off the phone," then carried on chatting to Grandma Jones.

Becky walked slowly outside again, camcorder at the ready, wondering how she could really convince them.

It was more than an hour later that her absence was noticed.

"She's probably still in the garden," said her mother.

She left the room and went to the door.

"I can't see her anywhere," she reported when she came back, "and she didn't answer when I called, either."

"I know where she'll be," said Grandma Herbert with some certainty. She went into the garden and made her way up the steps at the side of the rockery. When she came back, all she had was the camcorder in her hand.

"I found this propped up against a rock and pointing at the flower pots," she said ominously. "I think it's very careless of her."

Uncle Mike took the camcorder from her.

"She must have left it running. It's been on so long that it's rewound itself," he commmented as he examined it. "I wonder what on earth she could have been filming?"

"Show me how to plug it into the

television so we can all see," said Becky's father. "That might be amusing, don't you think?"

"I hope nothing's happened to her," said Becky's mother anxiously.

"Of course nothing's happened to her. She probably put it down then went round to Julie's next door to show off her party dress," said her father. "I'll give her what for when she comes back for leaving this outside."

Uncle Mike showed him where to plug it into the back of the television, then Becky's father switched it on and found the correct button on the remote.

"Now we'll be able to hear the sound as well as see the picture," remarked Uncle Mike as they stood round ready to watch.

On the screen appeared Becky's father's first shots of the party, and they could all hear what was being said. Then it changed to a shot of him walking in the garden and they could hear Becky telling him firmly what he had to do. Then they saw and heard Becky's mother calling from the door, and Becky's father hurrying back into the house.

Then the scene changed abruptly, first to the flower pots behind the cold frame on the other side of the rockery, then to at least half a dozen little figures which, after a few moments appeared cautiously out of them.

"Good gracious!" exclaimed

Grandma Herbert, clutching her chest.

But worse was to come. The next scene showed the same little creatures, exactly like tiny humans but dressed in a very strange way. And standing in the middle of them, to their horror, was the tiny figure of Becky!

"I told you they were real," they heard her say, in a high-pitched voice quite unlike her normal one. "Now you'll have to believe me."

Then she waved happily before darting back inside the plant pots with the rest of them. Shortly afterwards, the screen went blank.

DEAD BABY'S LEG

"**M**y sister's home again," announced Pete, in case anyone wanted to know. "She flew in last night."

The others were playing in the woods when he found them. They often went there when the weather was fine. Mark was up a tree while Jimmy and Ben were swinging from a branch on an old rope they'd found.

"Where's she been?" asked Ben.

"America this time," said Pete proudly.

"On holiday?"

"No. She's a model, remember? So she was working most of the time, wasn't she? But it wasn't half interesting, some of the things she's been telling me."

"Such as?" asked Mark, starting to

climb down. He hadn't been up very far. "Did she pose for magazines with no clothes on?"

"No, she didn't!" retorted Pete indignantly. "Like I keep telling you, she walks up and down at fashion shows showing off new clothes, that sort of thing."

They all knew that. Pete was always boasting about his sister. Mark was only trying to wind him up.

"Waste of time asking to see any photographs, then," said Mark.

"Coming in to land!" warned Ben.

He and Jimmy tumbled down together and landed in a heap.

"Ow! Nettles!" announced Ben. "So go on, what's she said that's so interesting?" he asked, rubbing his arm.

"Well ... " said Pete slowly, almost confidently, "for one thing, she says that in some places in New York now it's all the rage to eat people."

They stared at him in disbelief.

"She's having you on," said Mark eventually.

"Not whole people, of course," said Pete hastily, "just bits of them. And only at special parties, night clubs and things."

"She's got to be having you on. I mean, where could you get even bits of people from?" demanded Mark.

"Hospitals, places like that, apparently.

Arms and legs and things I expect. But it's very expensive, of course. Two thousand dollars a piece, I think she said."

"That's got to be rubbish," said Jimmy with certainty.

But then they considered.

"They eat chimpanzees in Africa," said Ben. "It was on the telly. And apes." He was inspecting his arm to see if a rash had come up yet. It hadn't.

"And come to think of it, some businessmen in China eat monkeys' brains," said Jimmy more thoughtfully now. "Apparently they stand round a table with a monkey's head sticking up through a hole in it, slice the top off then all dip in. With long-handled spoons!

They weren't sure they believed that either.

"Urgh," said Mark. "I'd rather be a vegetarian than do that."

"My brother once ate horse meat when he went to France," announced Ben. "He said it tasted sort of sweet. He didn't know what it was until they told him afterwards."

"I wonder what people taste like," said Jimmy even more thoughtfully.

"I expect it depends," said Pete. "I mean, some old woman's bound to taste different from a baby. And she'd be tougher, so she'd take longer to cook."

"I wouldn't fancy eating a bit of old woman," said Mark. "Nor a baby, for that matter. Anyway, babies smell funny."

"You'd wash it first, I suppose," said Jimmy, "before you cooked it. I wouldn't mind trying a finger, say, just to see what it tasted like."

"Cannibal!" Mark told him.

They decided to go home the long way round, and set off.

"But just imagine," enthused Jimmy, "going to the butcher's and asking for half a kilo of baby's leg, please, and my mother says make sure it's not more than a two-year-old! Perhaps they can in New York."

They looked at him. He was joking, of course.

They reached the end of the woods, climbed over the fence into the field and stopped cautiously for a moment. Against the hedge, just over to their left, an old man was bending over a fire.

They had never seen him before. He wore a long, scruffy coat which looked as if he had been sleeping in it. He probably had. He had built himself a little shelter of branches and twigs against the hedge.

While they watched he took a large knife from one of the big pockets in his coat and started poking at something in the embers with it. Obviously satisfied, he sliced off a piece of whatever it was, sat down in the entrance to his little shelter and casually ate it.

"What do you think it is?" muttered Mark.

"It's a tramp," Ben whispered back.

"No, I mean, what's he eating?"

They stared, trying to make it out. Something looked disturbingly odd about what was in the fire. It was sort of ...

"It looks like – no, it can't be," said Ben in horror.

They knew what he meant. It did look very like a small human leg, a bit plump in the middle.

At last the old man noticed they were watching him.

"Want a bit?" he called cheerfully, holding up his knife and waving it enticingly.

They approached, very cautiously, until they were a few safe paces from him. Since they didn't answer, the tramp went over to his fire, cut off another slice and held it towards them in his fingers invitingly.

"Come on, try some," he said. "You'll like it."

"What is it?" asked Mark suspiciously.

"Take a look at what I'm cooking," replied the tramp, "then you tell me."

They gathered closer round the fire and looked.

"Oh, it looks like rabbit," said Ben, rather relieved.

"So if it looks like rabbit, that's what it must be, isn't it?" said the tramp. "So who wants a nibble?"

Jimmy decided to risk it. The others watched.

"It tastes okay," he said in some surprise.

"So it should. Have you tasted rabbit before?"

"No."

"You haven't now, either."

"You said it was rabbit," accused Ben.

"I didn't. I only said it looked like one."

"But if it isn't rabbit, what is it?" asked Mark, peering into the fire again.

"Dead baby's leg!" said the tramp.

They ran. By the time they had raced to the gate at the far end of the field, scrambled over it and reached the safety of the road, they could still hear him laughing. When they paused, completely out of breath, and looked back, he was waving his knife at them again.

"Mr Hansen," urged Mark between gasps. "Let him sort this out. After all, it's his field. Come on!"

To their relief, the farmer was at home. He opened the farmhouse door and told them off for battering so hard on it.

"Rubbish!" he said sternly, once he had managed to sort out what they were all trying to tell him.

"But it's true!" said Mark rather desperately.

"Show me," said Mr Hansen picking up a heavy walking-stick.

They followed him rather nervously back along the road and into the field at the end of the woods.

"There he is," said Pete, pointing.

Only now the tramp was no longer by himself. They could see three other men with him. One of them was a policeman. Mr Hansen strode across his field towards them, while the boys followed rather more nervously behind.

"What have you been cooking in that fire, Henry?" they heard one of the men asking as they drew nearer.

"Only rabbit," replied the tramp, "But you can't have any. There's none left. I've eaten it all."

"So wouldn't you like to come home now?" asked the other man, obviously trying to persuade him.

"All right. But I'm going to put the fire out first," Henry said agreeably.

He started to stamp on it. The policeman turned and saw them.

"We don't need spectators," he said firmly.

"This is my field," retorted Mr Hansen. "What's going on?"

"Nothing to bother about, sir. It's just someone we've been looking for. I suppose these must be the boys Henry mentioned to us. Did he give you anything to eat?" he asked them.

"Jimmy ate some of it," said Ben.

"We thought it was rabbit. But then he said it was a dead baby's leg," admitted Jimmy.

The policeman looked rather uncomfortable for a moment.

"Um – yes. Of course it would be rabbit. Just his little joke, of course. The fact is, you see – well, Henry is someone who – er – escaped."

"Escaped from where?" asked Pete.

"Well, perhaps it's as well you were together when you found him, not on your own."

"Why's that?" demanded Ben.

"Just to be on the safe side. Not that he's ever done anyone any harm yet, of course. But you never know," said the policeman rather mysteriously.

Henry was still happily stamping all over the fire to make sure it was really out. Then he went to the hedge and started to flatten a patch of bare earth which happened to be there.

"Come on, Henry, that's enough," one of the men urged him rather sharply.

They watched him being taken to a

white van parked on the road at the other end of the field.

"Madman," said Mr Hansen. "That's it! Just make sure this hasn't given you boys any ideas about lighting a fire in one of my fields, that's all."

He strode off and left them to it.

"Of course it was only a rabbit," said Mark when he had gone.

"It didn't taste like rabbit," said Jimmy.

"How do you know? You said you'd never had any before."

"No, but somehow it didn't taste like I thought rabbit would," said Jimmy. "It was sort of different from what I expected."

"Uh-oh," said Pete.

They went to see what he had found. He was staring at the patch of earth, looking very much like a recently filled-in hole, which Henry had just trampled flat at the side of the hedge.

It was baby-sized. Big enough for about a two-year-old, by the look of it.

"So go on, Jimmy," Pete urged eagerly. "What did it really taste like?"

Now that had been sorted out, Jimmy wasn't reluctant to talk about it at all.

"Well," he explained, "I'd say it was more like chicken than anything, I suppose, only a bit sweeter. And it sort of felt soft when you first bit into it ..."

THE GREAT SALVO

Well, it had seemed a good idea at the time. Mrs Burrows had thought so, anyway. Mr Burrows had not been so sure.

"But it's Charles's birthday," said Mrs Burrows, enthusiastically, "and he'd love a party."

"But they'll be running all over the house," grumbled Mr Burrows, "making nuisances of themselves, probably being sick all over the carpet. We'll have to hire an entertainer as well! Is it worth it? Besides, are we sure Charles has that many friends?"

"Of course he has," replied Mrs Burrows. "Charles has lots of friends. Here's the list of those he wants to invite."

She showed him. It was even worse than he had thought. All of them right rascals, especially that one called Jake, thought Mr Burrows gloomily – and so many of them. Charles seemed to attract them like flies.

"But do we really need an entertainer as well?" he persisted. "I mean, couldn't we just ... "

"We're going to have a magician," said Mrs Burrows firmly. "He calls himself The Great Salvo. Maggie Simmons recommended him highly after her little Rachel's party a month or so ago. Anyway, I've already booked him for Charles's party next Saturday," she reminded her husband, as if he'd forgotten when his son's birthday was.

He brightened.

"Oh, will that be in the afternoon?" he asked hopefully.

"Three o'clock. Before they have their tea."

"What a pity it's going to be in the afternoon. I've already arranged to play golf. Sorry I shall miss the fun."

"That's quite all right," said Mrs Burrows, rather coldly. "We shall manage – as long as you've remembered to get him his present."

"It'll be here Saturday morning," Mr Burrows promised.

It was a mountain bike, just what Charles wanted. Though since there were no mountains where they lived, Mr Burrows didn't quite see the point! Still, if that was what the dear little chap had set his heart on ...

It arrived by special delivery on the morning of Charles's birthday. Charles ripped off the brown paper packaging at once and spent part of the morning riding the bike enthusiastically across the lawn and into the flower beds before announcing he was bored with it already.

Mr Burrows was just about to drive off to the golf course that afternoon when a dilapidated van turned up and an unhappy-looking man with a drooping moustache got out.

"Mr Burrows?" he asked. "I'm the entertainer for the children's party. The Great Salvo, genuine magician," he added, shaking hands. "It says so on the side of my van."

He pointed. It did.

"The best of luck," responded Mr Burrows. "They've all arrived. I've seen 'em. Frankly, I don't fancy your chances with that lot. I wouldn't like to try to entertain them myself, anyway. There must be easier ways of making a living."

Oddly, The Great Salvo brightened immediately.

"I like a challenge," he said. "I hate it when the children just sit there politely so I don't know whether I'm going down well or not."

He paused thoughtfully.

"Do I take it that you don't entirely approve of your child's choice of friends?"

"Not a single one of them," said Mr Burrows bluntly. "And to be honest, I don't always entirely approve of the little child himself. Charles can be a terror. And watch out especially for a boy called Jake. If anything, he's even worse."

"Thank you for warning me," said The Great Salvo. "Now I know how to entertain them as you would desire."

"Better you than me," said Mr Burrows. "I hope my wife paid you in advance, that's all." And he drove off as fast as he could.

The Great Salvo watched him thoughtfully as he left. Then he unloaded from the back of his van a large wooden box with a closed lid, followed by a large black holdall.

He unzipped the holdall to take out some striped canvas and several metal poles and carefully assembled them to form what looked like a little oblong frame tent.

Then he went back inside his van and changed into flowing robes and an ornate turban which he placed carefully on his head. When he stepped out again, he was totally transformed! Instead of being a little, unhappy-looking man, he now seemed

strangely taller, with a pointed black beard.
Even his moutstache no longer drooped.

Mrs Burrows came to the door at once.

"You must be the magician!" she
cried.

The Great Salvo eyed her scornfully.
She wouldn't have expected him to be the
milkman, dressed like that!

"Children, the magician has arrived!"
she called.

At once there was a rush to the door
from behind her. Charles and Jake were in the
lead. Charles regarded the entertainer with
some disdain.

"You look like something out of a
pantomime," he commented, rudely.

"It adds to the magic atmosphere,
young man," said The Great Salvo. "Most
people like it."

"I don't," said Charles bluntly.

"And that thing over there looks like a
toilet tent," observed Jake, pointing.

Two of the girls who had been invited,
Julie and Amy, tittered. Both were wearing
bright red lipstick. The Great Salvo glanced
round at the assembled mob of children and
understood exactly what Mr Burrows had
meant.

"I bet the whole show's crap," added
Jake, "To go with the toilet tent."

The girls' titters burst into uproarious
laughter at his witty comment and

immediately the rest of Charles's friends joined in. The Great Salvo regarded them with a secret smile on his face.

"We shall have to see, shan't we?" he said softly. He turned to Mrs Burrows. "And where would you like me to put my equipment, madam?" he asked smoothly.

"We could tell you," chortled Charles into more guffaws.

The Great Salvo, still smiling, ignored him.

"If you'll follow me, I'll show you where," said Mrs Burrows.

"We'll help you take your stuff inside," volunteered Charles, and he and Jake rushed forward to take hold of the wooden box.

By some strange accident, they managed to drop it as soon as they had picked it up. The lid opened and everything in it fell out in a heap.

"Oh, sorry," said Charles, grinning. "Is this supposed to be a stuffed rabbit, then? I suppose you're going to pull it out of this top hat later."

He picked them both up, stuffed the rabbit down into the hat, waved his spare hand over it and pulled it out again.

"See, anybody can do that," he remarked gleefully.

"I'd prefer to keep them in the box for the moment," said The Great Salvo, quietly.

Still smiling, he took his things from Charles and started to pick up the rest of his magic items and return them to where they belonged. "I shan't need any help from these delightful children, Mrs Burrows. Just show me where I am to perform, then give me a few minutes and all will be ready for their entertainment."

He closed the lid of the box firmly.

"Er, I don't think you should go inside there just for the moment," he remarked, noticing Jake trying to find his way into the little tent. "If you'll wait until later, I'll make it much more fun for you."

"Yes, all of you come inside, children," urged Mrs Burrows, "then go through and wait in the back garden until Mr Salvo's ready for you." Matters were now getting just a little out of hand, she could tell. "This is exciting, isn't it?" she added hopefully.

The magician followed Mrs Burrows and the stampede through the house.

"This will do very nicely," he remarked, looking round the large drawing room, which was already arranged with two rows of chairs facing a space which had been cleared at one end. He went out again to collect his magic tricks.

He could see a row of faces grimacing at him through the windows when he returned and began to set them up. About fifteen of them, as far as he could judge. He smiled to himself again as he placed his wooden box on a table which Mrs Burrows had thoughtfully provided, and stood the little tent by the wall in a corner, with its holdall on the floor at the side of it.

After a few moments he called through the door,

"I'm ready to begin the entertainment, madam."

Mrs Burrows didn't need to call them. They had already seen through the windows that the show was ready and were hurtling in and noisily scrambling for the seats. Charles pushed Julie off her chair at the front and sat on it himself, while Jake pushed Amy off hers to sit beside him. The chaos subsided very slowly.

The Great Salvo looked round the assembled group and nodded, almost as if to himself.

"You don't need to stay if you have more important matters to attend to," he said to Mrs Burrows, who was hovering anxiously at the back of the room.

"If you're quite certain you can manage by yourself," she said thankfully, and slipped out quickly before he could change his mind.

"First," he told his audience, "I shall start my magic with just three pieces of string. Watch closely."

He opened his wooden box to fish out the pieces of string, counting "one – two – three," as he brought each one out with his right hand and passed them one at a time to the other. When he flicked his left hand, he was now holding just one long piece of string.

He flicked again, and now there were three pieces of string knotted together. The third time he flicked his hand they separated again. He returned them to the box and bowed.

"You swapped them," said Jake. "You'd got the others up your sleeve all the time. I saw you do it," he lied.

"And now," said The Great Salvo, ignoring him, and with a flourish waved both hands in the air and produced a bunch of bananas out of nowhere.

"They were up his sleeve as well," called Amy.

The Great Salvo now drew their attention to two cardboard tubes which he took out of his wooden box. He turned them lengthways towards his audience so they could see right through them and so know they were both totally empty. Then he stood them upright on the table.

"Now watch," he said.

He picked up one of the empty tubes, and underneath it stood a full bottle of milk. He picked up the other tube, and there was a bottle of pop. He put the first tube down in a different place, when he lifted it this time a jar of jam stood there and when he lifted the second tube, a tub of ice cream appeared.

Soon all available space on the table was cluttered with different bottles, jars and containers as he carried on putting down each empty cardboard tube in turn then lifting it up again.

"I've seen that done before," remarked Jake loudly, "on the telly. It's an old trick. Call yourself a magician?" he added contemptuously.

Then The Great Salvo opened his mouth and started to pull out enormous lengths of green, blue, yellow and red coloured ribbons, which he collected in his hands. He then passed them through his teeth and they became little flags of all the nations, all fastened together, which he draped round the room. Still they were not impressed! Jeers and catcalls followed instantly.

Pulling a rabbit out of an empty top hat was not a success either, as far as the children were concerned, not even when it came out obviously stuffed, and then, after he dropped a black cloth over it, hopped out from under it quite clearly alive.

He dropped the cloth over it again and when he lifted it up the rabbit had completely vanished!

"That's gone up his sleeve as well," said Charles knowingly.

They even pretended not to be impressed when he produced a large empty bird cage out of thin air right in front of their eyes, without even a cloth to hide what he was doing. Nor when a live canary suddenly appeared inside it. Nor when he opened the door of the cage and it flew out to turn immediately into a bunch of grapes.

He made a little pencil turn into a full-sized walking-stick; he produced an egg from somebody's ear, and a ball-point pen apparently from up somebody else's nose. He did tricks with playing cards.

He told them all in turn when their birthdays were, apparently simply by shutting his eyes and concentrating, and followed that by describing accurately what was in everyone's pockets. He even borrowed a hankie from one of the girls, Julie, and made it float by itself all the way across the room and back again without anyone touching it.

It was all to no avail! Charles and Jake kept up their disparaging comments throughout the performance, and when they – occasionally – fell silent, the rest of them followed their example and took over.

Then The Great Salvo covered his large wooden box with a big black cloth, and when he drew it away the entire box and all its contents had completely vanished. He screwed up the black cloth, threw it into the air and that vanished as well. Now that was a surprise.

"Huh! When are you going to use that tent thing, then?" demanded Jake eventually.

"Yeah, what are you going to do with that?" called Charles. "You've just left it standing at the side of the room all the time so far."

"We want the tent, we want the tent," they all began chanting together.

The Great Salvo was not at all put out. He raised his hand for silence, and for once got it.

"I thought you'd want me to show you the tent sooner or later," he said quietly. "So now I shall oblige. You're all going to find this most interesting, I assure you."

"I bet we shan't," jeered Jake.

"No, we shan't," said Charles, grinning with him.

"Perhaps you two would like to inspect it first, then," The Great Salvo said, carrying the tent to the centre of the space where he was performing. "Come and take a careful look at it," he encouraged. "Make sure it's just an ordinary sort of tent."

He didn't even object when the two boys tipped it right over to peer inside.

"Now are you quite sure it's completely empty?" asked The Great Salvo, putting it upright again.

"Yep," said Jake.

"Just a stupid little tent," agreed Charles.

"Then perhaps one of you might like to stand inside it," suggested The Great Salvo.

"I will," said Jake. "Now what's supposed to happen?" he asked once he was behind the canvas with the flap closed in front of him.

"Kazzam!" said The Great Salvo.

Nothing happened.

"Okay, so now what?" asked Charles.

"You can go inside as well if you like," said The Great Salvo.

Nonchalantly, Charles strolled up to the tent, lifted the flap, and –

"Hey, it's empty," he announced in some surprise. "Jake's not there."

"Go right inside to make quite sure about that," urged The Great Salvo, so Charles did.

"Kazzam!" said The Great Salvo again.

Then he took the metal poles out of the tent, collapsed the canvas neatly into a small pile, stuffed the whole lot into its holdall and zipped it up.

"Thank you, ladies and gentlemen," he said to what was left of his surprised and horrified audience. "That is the end of the show."

After bowing deeply, he strolled out through the door with the holdall in his hand.

As Mr Burrows stepped out of his car after his game of golf, The Great Salvo was standing by his dilapidated van. However, he didn't seem as unhappy as when Mr Burrows had seen him earlier that afternoon.

"I think you'll find," said The Great Salvo, "that everything went just as you would have wished."

"Is the party over, then?" asked Mr Burrows, listening. "I certainly can't hear any shouts, shrieks or general mayhem inside the house."

"They've just had rather a big surprise," said The Great Salvo cheerfully, "so I think they're all keeping very quiet for the moment. You might need to have a word with Mrs Burrows before very long. I don't think she's quite realised yet precisely what the big surprise was."

Then he threw the holdall into the back of his van, slammed the door shut and drove off, whistling happily to himself after another job well done.

After all, Mr Simmons hadn't been too keen on little Rachel either, before her mother had hired him to entertain the children at her birthday party a month or so previously.

THE WINDOW

The old house was haunted, all right. Everyone knew that. It even looked haunted.

It was tall and gloomy-looking. There was a big old-fashioned chimney stack, windows which narrowed to a point and the sort of over-hanging eaves you might expect bats to fly out of. The black paint on its doors and window frames had been peeling for as long as anyone could remember.

It stood behind a high wall at the end of Knotts Lane on a little rise in the ground which made it seem even taller. It had, of course, been empty for years.

The house was so haunted, in fact, that at night no one ever dared open its creaking iron gate, even if there was someone else with them at the time. Everyone knew the gate creaked because every now and then, especially just as it was getting dark, somebody would push it open to see if it still did – and then run!

But whenever people did that, the next time they passed they always found the gate firmly shut again.

"It's got to be the ghost who comes out at night and shuts it again every time someone opens it," said Michael with certainty. "I mean, who else could it be?"

They were on their way home from school at the time. He clicked the latch and gave the gate a tentative push. It opened, creaking beautifully. But it was still daylight, so they didn't need to run.

"Perhaps somebody from one of the other houses along the road who doesn't like seeing the gate left open," suggested Jason.

"Would you shut somebody else's gate for them, then?" asked Michael.

"I might. Like, if the people next door had gone away, I might push their newspaper all the way through if I saw it sticking out of the letterbox."

They considered.

"I bet you wouldn't if this house was next door to yours," said Luke.

"Why not?" demanded Jason.

"Because then your next door neighbour would be a ghost, that's why not."

"But how does anyone know there

really is a ghost?" asked Jason pitifully.

They looked at him pityingly. He was new and hadn't been at their school very long.

"Look, even my brother won't go near it at night, and he's fifteen," said Luke. "There's something in there. It creeps round at night, trying to get hold of you."

"What for?"

"How do I know? It just does, that's all."

"But how can anyone know that, when nobody's ever been near enough at night to find out?" asked Jason, reasonably enough.

"People have heard things," said Luke.

"Oh yes?" What?"

"Strange noises, that sort of thing, said Luke vaguely.

"That's a load of rubbish, if you ask me. It's just an old empty house, that's all."

"You just go close up to it, then, and find out," said Michael.

"Okay," said Jason, to their surprise, "I will."

He flung his bag boldly over his shoulder and stepped through the gate. Then he stood on the broken concrete path which led through the overgrown front garden.

"Anyone coming with me?" he asked, looking round.

They shook their heads.

"We'll wait here," said Luke.

Jason walked all the way up the path, avoiding the vegetation which grew over most of it, until he reached the big bay window at the side of the front door. He rubbed a circle of grime off with his hand and peered inside.

"There's nothing much in there," he called. "Just those tatty old curtains at the window and a few bits of mouldy old furniture. Like I said, just an empty house. I'm going round the back."

He disappeared down the side of the building. After a few minutes he strolled back again.

"Nothing to it," he announced as he rejoined them on the pavement, leaving the iron gate open behind him. "The back door's locked, but I managed to get a window open," he added casually.

"You didn't go inside?" said Luke in horror.

"No, but I could have if I'd wanted to."

"I suppose you got away with it because it's still daylight," said Michael grudgingly. "I mean, you never see a ghost then, do you? They only come out when it's dark."

"It might not be a ghost," commented Luke. "It might be anything."

"Well, whatever is supposed to be there, it's not there now," declared Jason. "And I don't think there really is a ghost. It's just a – a rumour, that's all."

"I bet you wouldn't say that if it was dark," said Luke. "I bet if it was dark you wouldn't go anywhere near the place, like the rest of us."

"I'm not scared of the dark," retorted Jason. "It's the same as the light, only you can't see anything."

"Exactly," said Luke. "When you can't see anything, then you can't tell what's there until it's too late and it's grabbed you."

"You'd be able to see if you had a torch," Jason persisted.

"You go there with one later tonight, then, and see where it gets you. But when you shine your torch, watch out for the shadows on either side. Goodbye, Jason. Pity we shan't be seeing you any more."

"All right, I will."

Michael and Luke stared at him.

"You don't mean it?"

"Of course I mean it. All we have to do," he enthused as they set off home, "is wait until it gets dark, then go round the back, open that window I told you about, then go inside, take a look round, and come straight out again."

"*We*?" asked Luke bleakly.

"Well, why not? Just because

everyone else is scared doesn't mean we have to be."

"No, I can't tonight," said Luke quickly. "Got to go to my aunty's."

"Tomorrow night, then."

"No, we're going out somewhere else. My dad told me this morning," he added unconvincingly.

"It'll easily be dark by nine," remarked Michael thoughfully after Luke had left them to hurry home. "Are you quite sure you didn't see anything inside that house? Or hear anything?" he added.

"There's absolutely nothing to be scared of at all," Jason assured him. "How long's it been empty?"

"Ever since some old man died in it – of fright, everyone says. Years ago. That's all I know."

"There you are, then!" said Jason triumphantly. "Perhaps they're still trying to find his relatives to tell them. Or they've already found them but they don't want it. I wouldn't be surprised. I wouldn't want to live there either. Too dark and gloomy for starters."

Jason was very persuasive. Dark clothes, he suggested, would be best, so if there were other people around they wouldn't notice them so easily and wonder what they were up to. Besides, dark clothes wouldn't show up the dirt so much, and it was bound to be dusty in there after all that time.

They'd need a torch of course – one each, and would have to make sure they worked. He expected they would be the first to go up to the house at night, let alone go inside. They'd be able to boast about it afterwards.

"Okay," said Michael, nodding. "Meet you there about nine o'clock. I'll bring a whistle as well."

"What for?"

"If there's an emergency, we might need to blow it."

Jason said it wouldn't be necessary, but Michael said he was taking one anyway.

It was almost dark when they met later that night. Michael was a little alarmed right at the start. The iron gate was shut again. He was sure they'd left it open, but as Jason pointed out, that didn't mean anything. Nor did the fact that the gate seemed to creak louder than before as he opened it.

They crept carefully up the path and round to the back of the house. At last Jason switched on his torch and flashed it briefly along the downstairs windows.

"This one," he said, pushing at it.

As it swung open he scrambled up and climbed in. After some hesitation, Michael followed.

"I think you're right, we are the first to

ever come in here," Michael whispered nervously once they were both inside. "Sometimes people had gone round the back, the same as you did, but only in daylight. That's why the windows aren't boarded up. They never needed to be."

Jason shone his torch again long enough for them to see they were in the kitchen. It had paint peeling from the walls, rust marks in the sink and a big empty cupboard.

At the far end a door lay invitingly open.

"Here, ghosty, come on, ghosty," he called into the darkness beyond.

"Shut up," Michael said anxiously, edging back towards the window.

"Listen. Can you hear something?"

Michael listened carefully, holding his breath.

"No," he said in some relief.

"Neither can I," said Jason cheerfully. "Like I said, there's nobody here but us. So come one, let's explore while we've got the chance."

Michael plucked up the courage to follow him through the doorway into the passage beyond, and when Jason opened the door to the first room they came to and switched on his torch, they both looked inside.

There were a few old bits of broken

furniture, but that was all. The other room on the ground floor, at the front, was pretty much the same, apart from decaying curtains at the windows and a clear area on one pane of glass where Jason had rubbed at it to see inside.

They decided to go upstairs. At least, Jason decided to and Michael kept close behind him, since he didn't want to be left by himself. They opened the nearest door, found a bathroom which hadn't been used for years, and shut it again. The next was a bedroom with nothing in it at all. They closed that door behind them as well.

There was a brass bedstead against the wall in the next room with a dirty-looking mattress on it. They went inside to take a closer look at that.

"I suppose that's where the old man died," remarked Jason thoughtfully. "Though I don't suppose anything really came to get him. Like I said in the first place, it's just an old house, that's all."

He shone his torch round the rest of the room.

"Come on, let's see if there's anything in the last bedroom, then we'll go."

"Shush!" said Michael suddenly.

"Why? We're – "

"Shut up!" hissed Michael. "Listen!"

Something was coming, very slowly and quietly, up the stairs towards them, but it didn't sound like footsteps – or at least, not human ones. It was more of a strange hopping sound, one step at a time, with a pause in between.

Jason switched his torch off at once. At the same time Michael quickly closed the door then stood trembling behind it.

They were only just in time. There came a final hop at the top of the stairs, then silence. Whatever it was seemed to be waiting – or listening.

"What are we going to do?" Michael whispered fearfully.

"Just keep still," Jason whispered back. "Perhaps it doesn't know we're here."

Michael suddenly realised that Jason was just as scared now as he was.

There was a strange scratching sound from somewhere near the top of the stairs, like sharp claws against wood. Then another hop. Then closer to them more scratching. It sounded exactly like something hopping along, scratching at each door in turn and trying to get in.

This was no ghost, it had to be something far worse. And it was coming closer. It was scratching at the door of the room where they were now. They both held their breath. It scratched again. Then it stopped abruptly.

There was silence.

They waited fearfully behind the

door, hardly daring to breathe at all. Nothing happened. They still waited.

"What is it?" whispered Michael.

"How do I know?"

"But what shall we do if it comes in?"

Any moment now he was expecting the door to swing slowly open and whatever was outside to come inside and find them.

"I mean, those claws ... "

"Shut up, Keep perfectly still."

Still nothing happened. They still waited. Then came two more hops – away from them – another scratch, then more silence.

After almost a minute of silent panic, Jason pressed his ear close to the door. Then, very slowly, he eased it open a tiny fraction and peered through the crack.

"It's gone into the last bedroom," he whispered. "The door's open."

"When it comes back ... " Michael quavered, "what shall we do?"

The window was too high from the ground to jump. In any case, it probably wouldn't open. Michael tiptoed across and tried to open it anyway while Jason kept watch. He couldn't get the handle to move.

"There's only one thing we can do – run for it!"

Jason very slowly began to open the door.

"Ready?" he whispered.

Michael nodded. He didn't need to say anything. He fumbled for his whistle, found it and put it to his mouth.

"Okay – now!"

Jason flung the door wide open. They tumbled out of the room and dashed for the stairs, then hurtled down, Michael blowing his whistle as he went.

As they reached the bottom they were almost sure they could make out something coming after them, something big and birdlike, hopping rapidly down the stairs. In his panic the whistle dropped from Michael's mouth as, like Jason, he ran for his life.

They reached the kitchen window almost at the same time, scrambled through as fast as they could and landed in a heap in the yard outside.

"Come on!" yelled Jason as they picked themselves up.

He began to run.

"Michael, come on!" he yelled again as he reached the corner of the house.

But Michael seemed to be just standing there, peering at something near his feet. Then he shone his torch at it. Jason paused uncertainly, unable to decide whether to run back and drag him away or make his own escape while he still had the chance.

Suddenly Michael called to him.

"It's all right now," he said, "I think."

Jason rejoined him, very cautiously.

"This got thrown out of the window after us," announced Michael almost calmly, picking it up.

It was his whistle.

Then the window suddenly slammed shut.

"Okay, so I was wrong. It *is* haunted," decided Jason as they set off home. "But Luke was right, it's not a ghost."

No, it wasn't a ghost. They both agreed on that.

"I still don't think we should tell anybody, though," said Michael.

Jason agreed. Best not say anything. Or ever go near the house again, even in daylight.

For one thing, after they had come out through the gate it had suddenly creaked itself angrily shut again and the latch clicked firmly back into place.

MIRROR, MIRROR

Georgina really liked mirrors. She liked looking at herself in them. She was fascinated by them. Sometimes she would sit in front of her dressing table, hold her hand mirror behind her head and look at the images which appeared for half an hour at a time.

First she could only see the back of her head. Then, when she tilted the hand mirror slightly, a whole sequence of alternate faces and heads stretched into the distance, almost like a separate universe forming itself in front of her.

Once she'd been to a science exhibition where, in a corner, had been a very low entrance with a notice over it inviting people to step inside and count the images they could see. She had bent low, entered, then stood upright.

That had been brilliant! Inside this little room were three huge triangular mirrors tilted at different angles so that wherever she had looked she could see dozens of images of herself from the back, front and sides. She had stayed there for ages, just looking.

What was missing in her own room, though, was a really big mirror. The one on the dressing table was all right, as long as she was sitting down. The hand mirror was useful for checking her hair at the back. But there was no way she could see the whole of herself in one go.

Georgina happened to mention this one day.

"I see what you mean," said her mother. "A girl your age needs to be able to see herself full-length, to check that her clothes look right, for instance." She obviously approved of the idea.

"You've got a birthday coming up very soon," remarked her father. "We'll buy you one then. We'll go and take a look on Saturday."

They actually let her choose for herself. They went into all the department stores, but there was not one which she liked. Eventually they found a shop hidden away in a narrow side-street. They came across it by accident while walking from one department store to another.

They peered through the window. The shop was full of different kinds of mirrors. Some of them were hanging from the walls in ornate frames. Others were stacked against each other in various corners – but these were just plain mirrors designed to be screwed onto walls. Others stood by themselves on stands of various types.

"This might be just the place at last," murmured her father as they went inside.

"That one!" said Georgina excitedly, pointing as soon as she saw it.

It was a tall mirror which swung in a sturdy frame of dark wood with a heavy base fitted with castors. She hurried over to inspect it more closely.

"Can I help you?" murmured a man in brown overalls, coming over.

"How much?" asked her father.

The man in overalls told him. From the way her father nodded, it seemed the price was reasonable, although Georgina didn't actually hear what was said. She was too busy admiring herself in the mirror.

"That kind of mirror is called a cheval-glass," said the man. "But it's not new, you know. It's almost an antique, I suppose. Now I could show you a more modern one, over here – " and he began to walk to another part of the shop.

"No, I like this one," said Georgina. "I

think it'll be just right."

"If that's what you want," said the man, looking at her rather oddly. And so it was agreed.

It was delivered early the following week.

"Go up to your bedroom," said her mother, smiling, as soon as she came home from school, "and see what's arrived."

Georgina knew at once what it was. She hurried up the stairs and found the mirror standing in a corner of her room. The glass was still covered in thick brown packaging and the wooden arms and base wrapped in brown paper to protect it during its journey from the shop.

There was a little decorated label attached by a piece of string. She tore it off and read it. "With love to Georgina on her birthday," it said.

She dropped her school bag on the carpet and began to unwrap her gift at once. She knew straight away that she had made the right choice.

So now for the best place to put it. She began to move it around the room on its castors, trying to decide, pausing each time to inspect the result critically. Her mother watched with amused interest.

"You need to put it where the light from the window will fall on you," she advised. "After all, you want to be able to see yourself in it, not just look at the mirror."

That was sensible. Finally Georgina knew where it would look exactly right – at the side of the window, facing the door.

"There you are, then," said her mother. "Just what you wanted, isn't it?"

Georgina nodded. It certainly was.

"Thanks very much for my present," she said.

When her mother had left, she experimented. First she tilted the mirror backwards a little, so she could see only her head and the ceiling. Then forwards, so she could see herself from the waist down and the carpet. Then finally, because the mirror was so tall and wide, just about vertical because that was exactly right.

Then she stared into it, fixing her eyes on the image of herself. As she moved forward, so the image moved towards her. Of course. As she drew back, so the image drew back in turn. Naturally.

Then she stepped back a few paces to where she could still see the whole of herself and the door behind her. She began walking slowly towards her image, watching the two of them getting closer and closer, until finally they were staring into each other's eyes with her nose almost touching the glass.

Despite its age, the glass was so clear it was exactly like staring into the eyes of a real person. That was when she noticed something rather strange – only for the moment she couldn't quite make out what it could be.

She moved away a little, and glanced upwards into the mirror to see the ceiling reflected in it, and her reflection moved similarly. She looked down at her feet in the glass. So did her image. So far everything seemed to be as it should be.

Then she put her nose close to the glass again and once more stared into the eyes of her reflection, because that was where the strangeness, if it was really there, had seemed to be.

They seemed all right now, though, identical to her own, as had to be expected.

Just to check, she went over to her dressing table and picked up her hand mirror and examined her eyes in that. Then she returned to her new gift, still holding the hand mirror, where of course she saw her reflection in the mirror appear and do exactly the same.

But something still wasn't quite right. It seemed to be something to do with the look in the eyes. It was as if they somehow flickered a little. Whatever it was, it was certainly rather disconcerting!

She stared hard into those eyes now, deliberately keeping perfectly still. Yet, there was still the faintest movement in the glass, the slightest flicker which ought not to have been there. When she narrowed her eyes, though, of course her image did exactly the same.

Of course there was nothing wrong! It was just a trick of the light, even if it was only the middle of the afternoon. On the other hand, she began to have a little twinge of doubt about her choice now.

It was worse that evening, though, just before she got into bed. Everything was *almost* normal, but there was still a strange something ... it was almost as if her reflection was watching her.

She knew she was being foolish, but she decided to turn the mirror round, away from her, so she wouldn't be able to see herself getting under the bedclothes.

It just had to be something to do with the thickness of the glass, she decided just before she went to sleep. The man in the shop had told her parents that showed its exceptional quality.

Maybe. But it was very disconcerting all the same. Still, now she'd got her mirror, the kind she had always wanted, she was determined to be satisfied. She'd soon get used to it.

The trouble was, she didn't! In the morning, when she turned her mirror back to where she wanted it, everything was fine. She was able to examine herself beautifully before she set off for school.

But, that afternoon, when she went to her bedroom and walked towards the mirror and their eyes met, that impression of the faintest of flickers was back again. Now it was almost as if her reflection were looking her over, in some kind of contempt. That was exactly how it felt.

A different universe, that was the impression Georgina got. In there – out here – different! Rubbish of course. She watched herself move backwards and forwards in front of the glass. It really was rubbish. It was just a perfect reflection she was seeing, but so clear it was almost like looking into a different room which happened to be absolutely identical to her own. But back to front, of course.

She even found herself having to check that out now. It seemed to be back to front, anyway. Of course it was.

Over the next few days, however, she began to grow more and more nervous about it all. So she decided to try an experiment, just to convince herself everything was all right. It was Saturday afternoon, and it was raining, so she was staying indoors. She had owned the mirror now for less than a week.

She went up to her bedroom, opened the door – noticing carefully that precisely the same thing was happening in the reflection – closed it behind her, then drew up the chair which usually stood in front of her dressing table and positioned it just in front of the mirror.

Then she sat down in it, looking at herself.

She stood up. The reflection of herself in the mirror did the same. She sat down again. The image copied her exactly.

To be honest, she didn't really know what she was expecting to achieve by this, but having started ... She raised both arms towards the glass, then tilted her hands so the palms were visible, watching herself doing that. Then she lowered them again.

The image didn't. Instead, with its hands still raised, it got out of its chair and stood up.

Georgina blinked in astonishment, mixed with panic and horror. This couldn't be! She had to be imagining it. She stood up herself now and found that everything was as it should have been. There she was, with her arms outstretched before her, facing her reflection which was now doing precisely the same.

Okay, so she had imagined it! But she did stand still for a horrible moment, wondering how on earth she'd managed to believe that such a thing had really happened. Then she stretched her fingers out and pressed them against the mirror. Because the glass was so thick, she could see that her fingertips didn't quite touch those of her reflection.

Then they actually seemed to touch, to come into contact with each other. That was really surprising. Next, she felt hands grasping her, pulling her hands through the mirror as if they were being plunged into icy cold water.

She felt her face touching that of the image in the mirror; she saw the eyes right in front of her own. Then suddenly, they vanished.

Georgina felt that she must have fainted, just for a moment, for when she recovered she still saw her own bedroom in front of her as she gazed *from the inside of the mirror*.

She saw herself standing there and suddenly burst out laughing. She herself was not laughing, she knew that. Instead she was standing stock-still in sheer terror at the unexpected situation.

Her terror increased as she saw the girl in her room go to the chair in which she had so recently been sitting, pick it up by its legs in both hands and raise it high in front of the glass. She knew now exactly what this girl was going to do!

Holding the chair over her head, the girl smashed it with enormous force on the glass in front of her.

The last thing Georgina saw as the mirror shattered into broken fragments in front of her was the girl running to the door and opening it.

And the last thing she ever heard was the girl shouting downstairs ...

"Mummy, mummy, something terrible's happened. I've just accidentally broken my new mirror!"

CENTRE OF THE UNIVERSE

U uncle Albert was supposed to have had a nervous breakdown years ago at university. According to Ross's father, he had never quite got over it, but that didn't bother Ross, even if it were true.

He liked his Uncle Albert. For one thing, he always treated him like an adult instead of just a kid. For another, he was so clever that Ross never had any trouble with his homework. He had only to ask if he was stuck, no matter what it was, and Uncle Albert was always able to put him right and he knew a lot of jokes.

But even Ross had to admit that occasionally Uncle Albert did become rather strange. Usually it was because he had developed another of his obsessions about something or other.

When this happened, he would concentrate on nothing else, sometimes for months on end, until he had finally got it out of his system and become normal again.

That's what had obviously happened this time.

Uncle Albert suddenly burst into their house, ignored Ross's parents as if they didn't exist, and rushed into the back garden.

"Ross, are you busy?" he asked.

Of course Ross wasn't busy. It was Sunday afternoon. He was just kicking a ball against the wall at the time.

"Then come with me," called Uncle Albert, excitedly. "I've got something very important to show you."

His father came to the back door. Ross looked at him. His father nodded. Best humour him, he'd be over it all the sooner, the nod said.

Ross's parents had decided they didn't want Uncle Albert living with them, so they had found him a flat not far away, where at least they could keep an eye on him. That was where Uncle Albert was taking Ross now.

"I've been working on it for months," Uncle Albert babbled as they hurried along. "I only finished the final calculations less than an hour ago. I want you to be the first to know of my amazing discovery!"

The large table inside his flat at which

he usually worked at his crazy ideas, was piled with huge sheets of paper which he had fastened together with sticky tape.

"You have to look at this first," his uncle urged, opening up the first sheet.

Ross saw it was a chart of all the stars and planets. Across it, Uncle Albert had ruled lots of long straight lines at various angles to each other. He had scribbled very complicated-looking calculations all round the edge.

"Next I continued those lines on to this," said his uncle, now unfolding another large map, this time of the world. "See? And then I transferred them all to this. Accurately, of course."

Then he unfolded a map of Britain with all the towns and cities on it.

"So what do you notice about the lines now, eh?"

"They all meet at a point, more or less just over where we live," said Ross, wondering where all this was leading.

"Exactly! But this is where it becomes absolutely fascinating."

And with the air of a magician pulling a rabbit out of a hat, he opened up the last sheet. This was so big that it covered the entire table and he had to let all the other sheets drop on to the floor.

"I didn't believe it myself at first. So I did all the calculations again to make quite sure. Then I found they were all absolutely correct the first time. So now there's no doubt about it whatsoever."

Ross found himself staring at a plan, to an enormous scale, of his own street. His uncle must have persuaded the local council offices to let him have it specially, because that would be about the only place you could get one like that. The tiniest features were on it, even down to the shape of the gardens.

"You see what I mean now?" demanded his uncle in even more excitement.

Ross did. All the lines came to a point directly over his own house.

"But do you realise what it means?"

"Well, no, not really."

"It's the centre of the universe!"

"I don't quite see," said Ross doubtfully, "how the centre of the universe can be in our living room."

That was where all the lines seemed to meet.

He felt a little anxious about that.

"No, no," said Uncle Albert, impatiently. "It's not at ground level. It's in your roof, up through the trapdoor into your loft then left a bit. I calculated that as well, the last time I paid you a visit, when no one was looking. But don't go up there expecting to find it."

"Why not, uncle?" Ross asked, just to humour him.

"Because the centre of the universe is also the centre of absolute time and motion. So whoever stood in it would never be able to move again in any direction. Others might be able to carry them away, but they wouldn't ever be able to move again by themselves. They'd become – well, eternal, I suppose."

That was when Ross thought he ought to be going. Uncle Albert had completely flipped at last. A pity about that. He wondered how long it would be now before they came to take him away.

"Think!" Uncle Albert almost snapped at him. "How old is your house?"

It was quite old, actually. It was one of a pair of semi-detached cottages built several hundred years ago, though considerably extended and modernised since. They were supposed to have been built on the site of even older houses.

"Can you ever remember your roof leaking or needing mending?" his uncle demanded.

That really surprised him, now his uncle mentioned that curious fact. He had never understood why the people next door were always having problems with their old roof while theirs, which was exactly the same age, always looked brand new.

"That's because the centre of the universe is protecting itself," said his uncle. "And what, might I ask, do you think happened to the workman?"

Ross sat down rather nervously now. He knew which workman his uncle meant. His father had once asked someone to inspect the roof insulation because the bedrooms always felt cold.

They had shown him where the trapdoor was, then left him to it. An hour later they wondered what was taking him so long. They found the trapdoor still open, and his ladder, but no sign of him anywhere. Nobody had seen him since. They kept his ladder in the garage in case he ever came back for it, but he never had.

And now Ross came to think of it, uneasily, there was always the mystery of the television. The tall trees growing in the woods at the back of their house caused television interference in every other house on their road. All the neighbours had to fit their aerials on long poles to be able to see anything at all, or have cable television.

They didn't. Their aerial was attached low down on an old chimney stack and even pointed the wrong way. It shouldn't have worked at all, but it did – perfectly! They were also able to watch programmes nobody else could even find.

"So now you know why, don't you?" said his uncle, grinning happily.

Ross thought it best not to mention any of this to his parents. He knew they would only worry, but he did tell his friend Adrian, next day at school.

"Whoever heard of the centre of the universe being up in somebody's roof?" scoffed Adrian.

"But what if my uncle's right, and it really is?"

"There's one sure way to find out," said Adrian. "I suppose your parents still go shopping every Saturday afternoon? If they do, and you've still got that ladder, I can bring a torch."

Ross considered. Despite what his uncle had said, he didn't see how anyone could come to any harm just by looking. Besides, Uncle Albert could have worked it out all wrong, despite everything. And even if he hadn't, they should be all right if they were careful.

"About two o'clock Saturday, then," he said.

It was easy to take the ladder out of the garage and carry it up the stairs because it was made of aluminium and not very heavy. Ross went up first with Adrian's torch, lifted the trapdoor and peered inside.

Some time in the past, long before they had lived there, somebody had pushed together a few old planks to make a bit of floor big enough to stand on. Beyond that were thick wooden beams fairly close together with deep spaces in between.

He could see the other thick beams supporting the roof, and the wall of the house at each end. There didn't seem to be anything else, though, apart from thick black dust everywhere and, as his father had suspected, no roof insulation either.

"Is there anything?" asked Adrian.

"Doesn't look like it."

They changed places so Adrian could take a look.

"We'll have to go right inside," decided Adrian. "It's the only way we'll ever find out for certain. And we might as well, while we've got the ladder up here. We might not get another chance."

Ross hesitated.

"But what if the centre of the universe really is up there, only we can't see it? Then anything could happen."

"I don't see how it can be, not if we can't see it," retorted Adrian. "But if it is a bit to the left, like your uncle said, we'll be quite safe if we keep to the side 'til we've got past it."

Put that way, Ross found himself beginning to warm to the idea, then thought of another problem. It was absolutely filthy up there. When their mothers saw the state of their clothes afterwards, they'd have a lot of awkward explaining to do.

"We'll just wear our underpants," suggested Adrian enthusiastically. "Then if we get dirty, we can have a quick shower afterwards before your parents come home and nobody will know."

If their underpants got dirty they could always change them afterwards. Mothers never looked at underpants before they threw them into the washing machine anyway.

It was tempting.

"Okay," said Ross.

"Watch out for a bit to the left," Ross reminded him once they were both safely up.

They walked sideways for a few paces to make sure they kept clear of where it might be dangerous. Now they were stepping gingerly from beam to beam, each keeping one hand against the roof for support. Adrian switched on the torch.

"Don't slip," Ross warned. "I don't want to have to explain why there's a hole in the ceiling of the bedroom underneath."

They reached the end wall.

"There's nothing here at all. But I suppose we ought to take a look at the other end just to make sure before we go down again," said Adrian, starting to go back the other way.

Ross followed more cautiously a few paces behind.

"Not that we're going to find anything there, either," Adrian added, as they got nearer the trapdoor. "If you ask me, your uncle must be mad. And if you ask me, the centre of the univer- "

The torch went out. There was a sudden blinding flash. Adrian vanished.

When Ross stopped blinking, all he could see was a lump of what seemed to be solidified ash, like a decrepit old statue vaguely of the same size and shape of his friend. As he watched in horror, it slowly toppled over and rolled to the side of the roof.

Ross froze. Then plucking up courage he went over to it and touched it gently. It felt quite cold.

"Adrian!" he called, hoping to hear an answer from the darkness on the other side of the trapdoor.

He called again, but when there was no reply, he stepped very gingerly indeed round the edge, until he was standing at the trapdoor again. He sat down carefully with his legs dangling through the hole while he frantically tried to think what he ought to do now.

Of course, he could always just go down, close the trapdoor, take the ladder away and pretend that nothing had happened.

After all, nobody else was likely to go up again for a very long time, perhaps years. Or ...

He kept glancing back at the peculiar

statue, hoping it wasn't really there and that this had never happened. Then he discovered to his alarm that not only was it really there, but it wasn't the only one.

In the gloom he could see a second one, similar but bigger and taller, tucked close to the side of the loft. That must have been why they hadn't noticed it.

He stared hard at both of them. He suddenly realised that somehow they both looked terribly familiar.

Scrambling to his feet he went carefully over to where they lay and rather to his surprise found he could lift both of them easily. They weren't heavy at all. Now he knew exactly what he had to do.

He carried Adrian gently down the ladder, trotted down the stairs with him and out through the back door. He stopped and looked round cautiously. There was nobody to see, so it should be all right.

Then he ran with him up to the far end of the garden, where his father had fitted a gate so they could go into the woods which interfered with everyone else's television except theirs. He went along the path through the woods to the small field on the other side.

After he had dumped him there, he ran back to the house again to collect the other chunk of solidified ash. The third time he returned he was carrying his father's spade. He had already decided where to dig the two holes.

He placed Adrian upright in one and the missing workman in the other. He patted the soil down hard and replaced the turf, then inspected his handiwork. They looked just right!

This field was supposed to be a prehistoric site thousands of years old, or so all the archaeologists who turned up every now and then, kept saying. But even they had never been able to agree on why ten strange statue-like objects stood in a circle inside it.

Well, now there were twelve of them. Ross didn't know how the archaeologists would explain that. Although he did wonder what they would make of the one, apparently just as old as all the others, but which looked like a workman in overalls, and the other remarkably like a boy in his underpants with what might have been a torch sticking out of his hand.

Now he knew exactly where over the centuries they had all come from, but even if anyone asked, he was never going to tell them.

Then he ran back home, put the spade away, threw the rest of Adrian's clothes into the loft, had a quick shower and got dressed properly. After he had closed the trapdoor and put the ladder away, he went round to see his Uncle Albert.

After all, he had something really fascinating that he just had to tell him!

KATE

"I suppose you know your house is haunted," she said from the other side of the front gate.

He looked at her. A year or so older than him, perhaps, or maybe about the same age. He couldn't tell for sure.

"I'm surprised you moved into this house at all," added the girl standing on the pavement.

"You're talking rubbish," he told her.

"You wait and see, then," she said mysteriously. "You'll soon find out."

"Oh yes?" he said scornfully. "And when will that be?"

"Tonight, probably, when it gets dark. You might see him walking about in your garden. I'm Kate."

"Joshua," he said.

She was wearing a white dress, almost as if she was going to a party. He hadn't seen her before, but then, they'd only moved in that day and he had been sent out into the front garden while his parents sorted the last few things out indoors.

"So I suppose that tonight, as soon as it gets dark, you're going to nip into our garden then wander about in that dress pretending to be a ghost," he said.

"Not me. And your ghost's not in white. He always wears dark clothes."

"So how does anyone see him, then, when it's dark? Come to think of it, how do you know there's a ghost anyway?"

"Of course you can see him," said Kate. "Why do you think the last people who lived here, left so quickly?"

Well, he knew the people before them hadn't stayed very long. He'd heard the estate agent telling his father that. The previous owners had completely redecorated the house as soon as they had moved in, but then they'd both got jobs somewhere else and had to move.

"So why did they?" he asked, casually.

"Because the ghost started going into the house," she replied, just as casually, "and Mrs Williams couldn't stand it any more. They lasted – oh, only about three or four months, that's all."

"And what about the people who lived here before them?"

"About six months. And the ones before them ..."

"I don't believe you," he said flatly. "And anyway, if he turns up in our front garden ..."

"It's not the front garden, it's the one at the back. And I don't care whether you believe me or not, I'm just telling you," she said as she ran off.

"A girl's just been telling me our house is haunted," he announced when he went back in. "She says it's a man in dark clothes who walks around our back garden when it gets dark."

"You'll be able to see him, then," said his mother affably, "since your bedroom's at the back."

At the time, she and her husband were moving the dining room table to where she really wanted it.

"Aren't you bothered?" Joshua demanded.

"No. And neither should you be. What nonsense! Do you want to believe everything some strange girl tells you? Now go upstairs and get your own things sorted out. I'll come up and see what I think when you've finished."

It had been a long day. They had been up at six that morning to be ready for the move. Joshua eventually went to bed early that night, without complaint for once, but before he got into bed, he drew back the curtains and peered out, just casually, just in case.

Then he dropped the curtains, hurried to turn out the light so his room was in complete darkness and lifted an edge of the curtain and peered out again. A man was walking slowly, in the dark, across the lawn and towards the house.

At first he thought it was his father, but it couldn't have been. For one thing, the figure was smaller than his father, sort of hunched and wearing dark clothes!

He watched, fascinated. The figure was walking, almost stumbling, closer and closer. Joshua pressed his forehead against the glass until the figure had just about reached the corner of the house. Then, very quietly, Joshua opened the window to get a better view.

The trouble was, by the time he had put his head out, the figure had vanished.

"Did you see him?" asked the girl. She was standing around outside on the pavement the next morning, obviously waiting for him to come out.

"Yes," he said, gruffly.

"Show me where he was, then," she said. So he opened the gate and let her in.

He led her along the path and through

the back gate. He was just telling her where the ghost was when his mother emerged from the back door, carrying some rubbish to the dustbin.

"This is Kate," he introduced. "She's the one who told me about the ghost."

"Oh yes?" said his mother, grimly.

"Well, I'm sure I really did see him!" he exclaimed. He'd already told his parents at breakfast.

"You think you did."

"I'm just showing her where I thought I saw him, then."

"You don't live next door to us, do you, Kate?" said his mother abruptly.

"No. I come from further along the road."

"That's what I thought. So if you don't live next door, how do you know what happens in our back garden?" demanded Joshua's mother.

Joshua hadn't thought of that, but the explanation was soon forthcoming.

"Everyone round here knows about it," Kate replied smoothly. "So I thought I'd better warn Joshua in case he saw it as well and didn't realise what it was." And she smiled sweetly up at Joshua's mother.

"I see. So it's just a rumour. Well, you convinced Joshua, at any rate. Do you know who this ghost is supposed to be?"

Kate shrugged.

"She told me he comes into the house sometimes," Joshua remembered. "That's why the last people who lived here decided to leave."

"Yes. Well, I think it's time you went now," his mother said to Kate. "Joshua's still not sorted out everything in his room yet, and he might as well do it now as later. Come along, Joshua."

He was up in his bedroom, sorting out his books and games, when he heard his mother suddenly shout angrily ...

"Get out! What do you think you're doing in here?" Then there was a thump!

He dashed down to the kitchen to find her locking the back door.

"Your ghost," she announced, sarcastically, "has just wandered right inside the house. I thought I heard something while I was in the front room. I wondered who it could be since I knew you were upstairs, and I found him just about to wash his hands at the sink."

"What was the thump?"

"I picked up the vacuum cleaner to hit him with it, but caught the edge of the door instead."

"Was he wearing dark clothes, and sort of stumbling as he walked?" asked Joshua.

"Yes. I'm going to tell your father we need a security light at the back of the house.

We don't want a tramp wandering around outside at night."

"But it's not night-time now."

"So he's not exactly a ghost, is he? He's just an old tramp, and if I see him around here again, I shall call the police."

Joshua unlocked the back door and shot outside. Whoever he had been, he was no longer there – or anywhere.

He dashed through the back gate to the front of the house and looked up and down the road. No one was in sight.

"He's gone," said Joshua when he returned.

The question was, where had he gone? He didn't think the figure he had seen walking so slowly could have run off down the road.

Later, his mother went out shopping, leaving strict instructions he was to keep the back door locked. Then, through the front windows, he noticed Kate at their gate again. He beckoned and she walked up the path to the front door.

"He's just some old tramp," he said bitterly as he opened it. "My mother found him in our kitchen not long ago."

"Can I come in and see?" Kate asked eagerly.

"If you want, I suppose."

He let her in. She walked straight into the kitchen and looked around.

"I suppose the back door would have been shut at the time, so he walked right through it as if it wasn't there at all," she commented.

"No, he didn't. He walked in when it was wide open," said Joshua. "It's locked now, though," he pointed out.

But when he turned round, Kate was no longer there! Puzzled, he went into the front room to find her staring out of the window.

"You shouldn't wander about in other people's houses without asking," he said sternly.

"Sorry, I wasn't thinking. I've been in this house lots of times before, that's why. Well, I'll be going now."

The trouble was that now she kept turning up at any old time, making excuses to come inside the house. It wasn't as if he particularly liked her, after all, but he hadn't made any new friends yet, since school didn't start for another few days.

The old man in dark clothes regularly stumbled his way across the back garden, always at about the same time in the evening. Joshua kept seeing him from his bedroom window.

He decided it might be best not to mention him to his parents again, especially since they hadn't put up the security lights yet. After all, he seemed harmless enough.

112

Even if he really was the famous ghost, he didn't see what the fuss could be about, nor why anyone should want to leave just because of him.

Anyway, he probably wasn't a real ghost, but just a tramp, who used their garden as a short cut. It would be easy enough for almost anybody to climb the fence at the far end of the garden and walk through to the street at the front, after all.

Their next-door neighbour rang the doorbell one evening. They already knew her name, and that she lived by herself.

"Are your parents at home?" she asked Joshua when he answered the door.

"It's Mrs Happs," he called.

His father appeared at the living room door.

"Come in, Mrs Happs," he greeted her. "Would you like a coffee? We're just about to have one."

"No, thank you. I'm not staying long, but I thought I'd better call round," she said as she followed him into the room. "I didn't like to come before, not until you'd got yourselves settled, so to speak. I know how it is when you've only just moved in."

She was invited to make herself comfortable in the armchair. She sat in silence for a moment.

"What I've come for," she said, hesitantly – "well, you've probably heard by now that your house is haunted."

"Oh, you mean that old tramp," said Joshua's mother. "Would you believe, I actually found him in the kitchen, almost as soon as we got here."

"Oh no, not the tramp," said Mrs Happs. "He's quite harmless, just simple in the head. When you see him again, just tell him to clear off or you'll tell the warden, and he'll soon go."

"The warden?"

"The man lives in an old folk's home, I suppose you'd call it, about a quarter of a mile from here, but unlike most of the others he's a little bit – well, different, shall we say? But unless you stop him you'll find him using your garden as a convenient short-cut several nights a week. He always tries it on whenever new people move in."

That rather disappointed Joshua at any rate. So he wasn't really a ghost after all!

"No, there's something much worse, and that's why I've come to warn you. You mustn't invite it into the house. But if it ever does get in, drive it out again and you should have no more trouble. Be as harsh as you like. Those who lived here before you couldn't bring themselves to do that, and by the time they tried, it was too late. That's why they had no option but to leave – in a hurry. Though I did warn them, the same as I'm warning you."

Joshua's mother was looking at Mrs Happs rather oddly now.

"What are you talking about?" she asked bluntly.

Joshua recognised that tone of voice.

"Oh, perhaps you haven't seen it yet, then. But you will. You certainly will before long."

The door bell rang again. Joshua went to answer it.

"Hello, Joshua," said Kate. "Can I come in?"

"I suppose so," he said, opening the door wider. "We're in here."

He closed the door and went back into the living room, expecting her to follow him. But she didn't. She seemed to be waiting outside.

"The ghost is a girl," Mrs Happs was saying. "She was rather a pretty girl, but quite mad. This is where she used to live, oh, years ago, just her and her father. One night, she tried to murder him while he was asleep by turning on all the gas without lighting it, but he woke and escaped in time. She ended up gassing herself instead."

"What was her name?" Joshua asked, fearfully.

"Kate. So if a young girl of that name ever persuades you to let her into the house, drive her out again at once, no matter what you have to do. What's worse is she appears in daylight, so you'd never suspect she was a ghost at all."

In a panic now, Joshua slipped back into the hall. The girl was no longer there. He looked first in the dining room and then the kitchen. She wasn't in either of them. He dashed off up the stairs.

"Hello, Joshua," she said, standing in the middle of his bedroom.

"Get out!" he ordered.

"And how are you going to make me do that?"

Mrs Happs, quite uninvited, must have followed him up the stairs and now appeared in the doorway.

"I thought so," she said grimly.

She rushed in, picked up his heavy bedroom chair and brought it crashing down over Kate's head!

Kate shrieked, but not out of pain or panic. It was a shriek more of sheer rage, and to Joshua's astonishment she was obviously totally unharmed. Then she slowly seemed to fade, and the shrieks died away, and she had vanished!

In silence, Joshua and Mrs Happs descended the stairs again, to find his worried-looking parents standing at the foot.

"I don't think you'll be troubled any more now," remarked Mrs Happs cheerfully. "But if you are, your son knows exactly what to do now. Don't you, Joshua?" she said.

He nodded.

"But – " he stammered when he was at last able to speak – "she said she came from further along the road."

"But she does, dear," said Mrs Happs, smiling at him. "Haven't you realised yet? Further along the road is the cemetery."

As she reached the door, she turned.

"Oh, by the way, if that old tramp does come along again don't be too hard on him. He wasn't always a tramp, you know. He was her father. He probably still thinks he lives here."

THE BEDROOM HORROR

"You're scared," she said

"No, I'm not. I'm not scared at all," lied Tom.

"Well, you look scared, anyway. And if you're not, why won't you go inside that room?"

"Well, I do go in. Sometimes."

"But only in daylight. You never go in there when it's dark, like it is now, do you?"

That was true. It was a pity she'd noticed, though. He hadn't realised until now that she actually had.

"You never go in there, either," he defended himself.

"Yes I do," replied Julia. "Lots of times."

"I've never seen you. So go on then, let me see you do it now."

They were standing in a dark passageway just outside the door of the room at the time. The entire house was very old, with the oldest parts of it dating back several centuries and this bedroom was said to be one of the oldest rooms of all.

They both knew what was supposed to be in there. There had been rumours for years. Now they were standing in the passage outside where it was really and truly dark!

Tom didn't mind the dark, but what he did mind was what he might find in the dark inside that terrible room.

"All right, I'll do it!" decided Julia, and went in.

After a few moments she came out again.

"See?" she said. "Nothing to it. Nothing happened to me at all."

"You didn't stay inside for very long, though did you?" said Tom, doubtfully.

"I could if I wanted to."

"Go in again, then, while I count to a hundred," he said.

Julia promptly went into the room again, and Tom began to count, very slowly.

"Ninety-nine, one hundred," he called eventually.

Julia came out, very casually.

"See anything?" he asked.

"Maybe," she said mysteriously. "Anyway, I'm not a scared little baby like you, even if there was anything."

"I'm not a little baby!" he said indignantly.

"Then prove it. You go straight in there now, the same as I did."

"How long for?" he asked nervously.

"Until I tell you to come out again. Go on, prove you're not scared," she said, contemptuously. "If you don't I'll tell everybody," she warned.

"Yes, but what if it gets me?"

"Of course it won't get you," she said with certainty. "And even if there really is something in there, no one's ever come to any harm before."

Tom knew that was true. When his cousin James had spent an entire night in there, for a dare, he had said it had been a complete waste of time. Nothing had happened whatsoever.

On the other hand, when Mary, one of Julia's friends, had once stayed there, she had rushed out screaming. It had been horrible, she said, and she'd never set foot in their house again.

She wasn't able to describe exactly what she had seen, because she'd run out so fast, but from what they could make out, it was something to do with a white figure, and groans, and big bulging eyes.

Her mother had been round to complain afterwards.

"Well – I'll have to think about it first," he said, playing for time. "How about tomorrow night?" he suggested.

"No. You'll do it now," she said firmly.

The old grandfather clock down in the hallway struck the hour slowly and solemnly. Well, it was late, but not all that late. Perhaps it would be all right.

He'd have to do something, even if only to shut her up. Otherwise she'd go on and on about it. Anyway, he would only need to do it just the once, to prove he wasn't really scared. But he was scared, all the same. He came to a reluctant decision.

"Oh, all right, if I really have to."

"But you're not to come out again until I tell you," she reminded him.

He nodded glumly. He wasn't happy about that either, but he really had no choice, now that he'd agreed.

Julia waited outside in the passage as Tom entered the room and the thick wooden door closed firmly behind him.

First he stood quite still for a moment in the gloom, just looking round the large, old bedroom. Directly opposite, in front of the big windows with the old curtains drawn across them, stood an antique dressing table with a huge mirror on top.

To his left, an enormous double wardrobe in dark wood reached nearly as high as the ceiling. To his right he could see, vaguely, a Victorian brass bedstead with the head of it against the wall and a low table at the side of it. An old fireplace, no longer in use, was nearby.

It was really eerie in there, no matter what anyone said. Tom didn't really like being there even in daylight, if truth be known. It was creepy even then, perhaps something to do with the heavy brocade curtains, the old dark furniture and the dismal-looking wallpaper which had been on the walls for years. And there was a peculiar smell as well.

He walked towards the curtains now, slowly and carefully. He'd do that, then walk back to the door again, just to prove to himself that he could. He made no sound on the rather worn carpet. He hoped Julia was still standing outside the door, just in case.

He wouldn't put it past her to have run off down the stairs, or into another room, or something, leaving him all by himself. Still, in the circumstances it wouldn't do to poke his head out just to see if she was still there. He'd have to stay in there until she called now, no matter what.

It was boring, really, he decided after a while. Perhaps the rumours weren't really true after all. Perhaps Julia's friend, Mary, had simply had an overwrought imagination the night she'd stayed there. Perhaps there was nothing to be scared about at all.

Tom grew bolder. He decided to walk right up to the bed now and touch the bedclothes, just so he could say that he had.

Then it happened! To his horror, as soon as he had touched them, *from the bed itself* he could see a figure slowly rising. What was worse, it was looking directly at him!

Horrible staring eyes bulged in its deathly white face. Then the figure's mouth opened and from it came a really scaring gasping sound then a horrible, cavernous groan.

Tom backed away rapidly. His worst fear, the thing he had always dreaded, was actually happening to him! Mary couldn't have been mistaken after all. She had really seen something as well! It wasn't just a rumour at all. This was horribly real!

The figure in the bed remained completely still for a moment, obviously watching him. Tom looked towards the door anxiously. He suddenly realised he had made a terrible mistake. He had backed away towards the windows. If this – thing – moved, it could come between him and the door. Then he wouldn't be able to get out.

Then, to his horror, the figure did move. It rose, very slowly, from the bedclothes, then from the bed, and began to move silently over the carpet towards him, hands outstretched threateningly.

Tom really panicked now. He had no

idea of what he should do for the best. There was no obvious way of escape. And shouting would be completely useless.

Then he realised that it was not coming straight towards him after all, but instead moving silently towards the bedside table. He stood still now, watching even more anxiously what it might do next. He distinctly saw a pale hand slowly reach out for the low table, then rise again with something clutched in it.

It was the heavy old candlestick which always stood there. He was sure that was what it was.

The hand rose higher, and suddenly let fly. Tom ducked as the candlestick hurtled past his head. Then he ran for his life! He rushed through the door to find, gratefully, that Julia had not left him alone after all.

"Run!" he shouted, breathlessly. "It's horrible, just like Mary said. He nearly got me. And now I think he's coming after us!"

Julia paused just long enough to realise to her horror that Tom really was telling the truth. The door was already creaking slowly open behind them. There really was a live human in there!

Then the two scared ghostly children dashed along the passageway and through the walls to another part of the house where they hoped they were safe.

Other titles available in the *SCARUMS* series ...

	ISBN	COVER PRICE
Sleep Well	1 84161 030 5	£2.99
The Ghost Train	1 84161 032 1	£2.99
The Werewolf Mask	1 84161 033 X	£2.99

Available from all good bookshops, or direct from the publisher. Please send a cheque or postal order for the cover price of the book/s, made payable to 'Ravette Publishing Ltd' and allow the following for postage and packing ...

UK & BFPO	50p for the first book & 30p per book thereafter
Europe & Eire	£1.00 for the first book & 50p per book thereafter
rest of the world	£1.80 for the first book & 80p per book thereafter

RAVETTE PUBLISHING LTD
Unit 3, Tristar Centre, Star Road, Partridge Green,
West Sussex RH13 8RA